KIDS' SPORTS STORIES

READY, SET, SWIM!

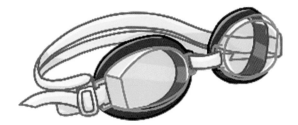

by Elliott Smith

illustrated by Katie Kear

PICTURE WINDOW BOOKS
a capstone imprint

Kids' Sports Stories is published by Picture Window Books, an imprint of Capstone.
1710 Roe Crest Drive, North Mankato, Minnesota 56003
www.capstonepub.com

**Library of Congress Cataloging-in-Publication Data is available
on the Library of Congress website.**
ISBN 978-1-5158-7097-5 (library binding)
ISBN 978-1-5158-7285-6 (paperback)
ISBN 978-1-5158-7131-6 (eBook PDF)

Summary: Sibling rivalry gets even more intense when twins are involved! Brothers and swim teammates Ty and Tristan have always tried to one-up the other, especially in the pool. When their competitiveness threatens to cost the team the big relay race, the swimming twins need to rethink, reset, and work together to bring home the win.

Designer: Ted Williams

Printed in the United States of America.
PA117

TABLE OF CONTENTS

Glossary

 **goggles**—special glasses that fit tightly around the eyes to keep out water

 **meet**—a swimming contest between two or more teams

 **relay**—a race in which four swimmers work as a team

Chapter 1
RULE THE POOL

"I think I'm the fastest," Ty said, spinning his towel above his head.

"No, I'm the fastest!" Tristan said, snapping his goggles.

The twin brothers were walking to swim practice. They loved sports. And they loved to battle over who was the best.

Ty and Tristan always tried to top each other. At every practice, they tried to beat each other in the final race. Today, they were excited about the next swim meet.

"I am going to swim last in the relay,"
Tristan said. "That's where the fastest
swimmer goes!"

Ty jumped in front of his brother. "You
know I'm the fastest!" he shouted. "I'm
going to swim last. I'll help us win."

The pool was just half a block ahead.

"Let's race to the gate," Ty said. "The winner gets to go in the pool first!"

The brothers took off running. They ran side by side. At the gate, they reached for the latch at the same time.

Practice was about to begin. The brothers changed into their trunks. Then they went to the pool deck. They were still talking about who won the footrace.

Coach Benjamin was waiting for them.
A girl their age stood next to him.

"Ty, Tristan, how are you?" Coach said.
"I want you to meet someone. This is Kat.
She is joining our team."

Ty and Tristan looked at each other.
A new swimmer?

Chapter 2

FAST AND FASTER

Kat smiled at the brothers. "Hi, guys. Nice to meet you," she said. "I'm happy to be on the team."

Coach Benjamin blew his whistle. "Everyone in the pool!" he shouted.

Ty and Tristan kept a close eye on Kat. She was fast. It didn't matter how fast they were. Kat was faster.

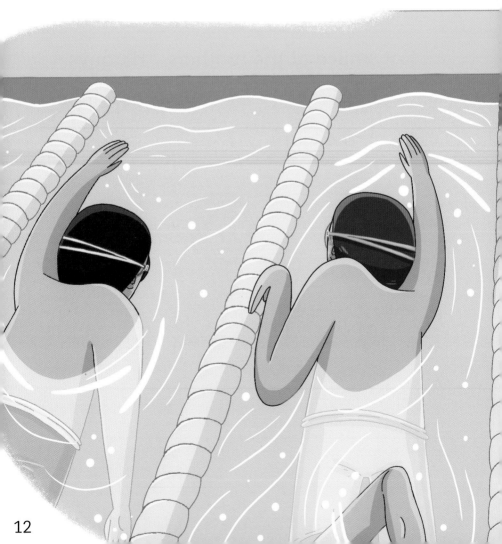

The brothers swam side by side. They reached the end of the pool and stopped.

"What does this mean for the meet?" Ty asked.

"We are the best swimmers on the team," Tristan said. "Don't worry about it."

Coach Benjamin called the team over.
It was time for the final race. That's how
Coach ended every practice. Ty and Tristan
nodded at each other. This was where they
proved who was fastest.

"Team, we have the big meet tomorrow,"
Coach Benjamin said. "Today's last race is
important. The first four finishers will be on
tomorrow's relay team."

The swimmers lined up at the edge of the pool. Ty and Tristan took their normal spots next to each other. But then Coach Benjamin put Kat between them!

TWEET! The whistle blew. The racers dived in. Everyone swam as fast as they could.

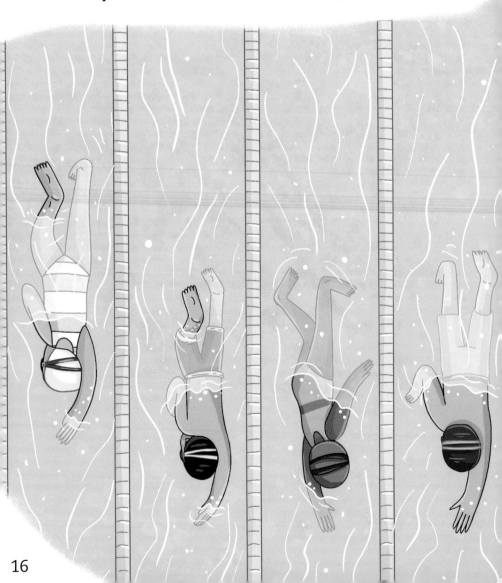

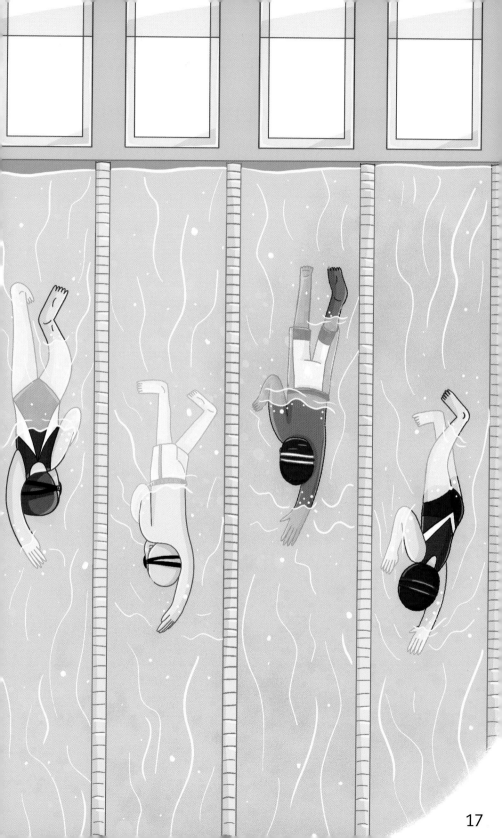

Ty's arms chopped through the water.
His brother's arms chopped just as fast.
Ty and Tristan swam hard. But so did Kat.
She kept up with them.

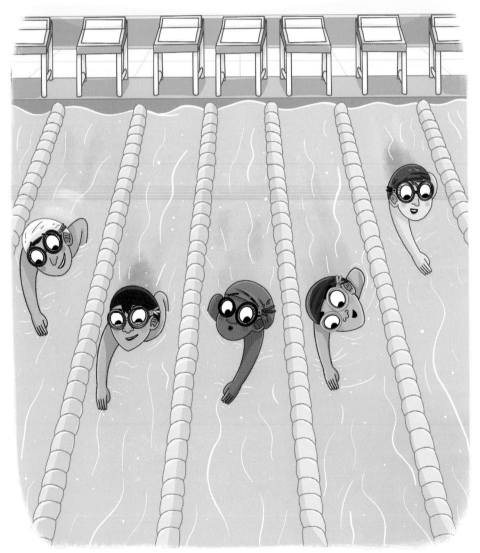

The two brothers reached for the wall.

Ty could see Kat's hand reaching out too.

"It's a tie!" Coach Benjamin said. "Great job, everyone!"

Coach pulled Ty, Tristan, Kat, and Brian aside. "I want you four to be tomorrow's relay team. Who wants to swim last?" he asked.

The kids all raised their hands. Coach pointed to Ty, Tristan, and Kat. "You three tied in the final race," he said. "Tomorrow, I'll let you choose who swims last."

Chapter 3
TOTAL TEAM EFFORT

At dinner, Ty and Tristan hardly ate.
They were very quiet.

"What's wrong, boys?" their mom asked.
"Most nights, you can't wait to tell your
dad and me about practice."

The twins told their parents the story.
They both wanted to swim last in the relay.
But Kat was a good swimmer too.

"I want to be the fastest!" Tristan said.

"But I think Kat beat us."

"Barely," Ty said. "She barely beat us.
But she did beat us."

"Coach didn't see it," Tristan said.

"It's not always about being the fastest, Tristan," the boys' dad said. "It's about what is best for the team. I know you and Ty will make the right choice."

It was the morning of the race. Ty and Tristan found Kat and Brian by the stands.

"Hi, guys," Kat said. "Since I'm new on the team, one of you should swim last."

Ty looked at Tristan. "We talked about it," Ty said. "You're the fastest swimmer. We think you should swim last, Kat."

"Brian wants to swim first," Tristan said. "I'll go second. Ty will be third."

"Great teamwork!" Coach Benjamin said. He had been listening all along. "Now let's put our hands in. One, two, three . . . go, Dolphins!"

The relay came at the end of the meet. Brian, Ty, and Tristan swam well. But the Dolphins were tied with two other teams. Then it was time for the last swimmers. They dived in. Kat took off like a rocket.

Ty and Tristan smiled at each other. They yelled for Kat. She moved ahead of the other swimmers. Their relay team won!

"We're all the fastest!" Ty said as the Dolphins cheered.

MAKE A MEDAL

Celebrate Ty and Tristan's team win in the relay race by making a first-place medal!

What You Need:
- a piece of construction paper, any color
- a yogurt lid
- crayons or markers
- safety scissors
- ribbon or string
- tape

What You Do:
1. Trace the lid on the construction paper with a marker.
2. Use the crayons or markers to make a design on the medal. Or color the medal gold.
3. Cut out the medal.
4. Shape the ribbon or string into an upside-down U shape.
5. Attach the string or ribbon to the back of the medal with tape.

Take another look at this illustration (when Ty and Tristan choose Kat to swim last). What do you think Kat is feeling during this moment? What do you think Coach Benjamin would have done if the team couldn't decide?

Now pretend you are Ty and Tristan. Write a letter to your grandparents that tells them about the big swim meet.

ABOUT THE AUTHOR

Elliott Smith is a former sports reporter who covered athletes in all sports from high school to the pros. He is one of the authors of the Natural Thrills series about extreme outdoor sports. In his spare time, he likes playing sports with his two children, going to the movies, and adding to his collection of Pittsburgh Steelers memorabilia.

ABOUT THE ILLUSTRATOR

Katie Kear is a graduate of the University of Gloucestershire, England, with a degree in illustration. Reading has always played an important part in Katie's life, and it was her deep love for books that made her choose a career in illustration. When she's not drawing, Katie enjoys adventures in nature, chocolate, stationery, the smell of cherries, and finding new artists to inspire her.